*I expect you have often heard people say someone was as fierce
as a wolf, as timid as a rabbit, as sly as a fox
or as wise as an owl.*

But not all wolves are fierce, any more than all foxes are sly
or all owls wise. It is as silly as saying all girls
are pretty or all boys brave.

This story is about a wolf who was not a bit fierce
and an owl who was very, very silly.
It is called. . .

THE STORY
OF THE KIND WOLF

Peter Nickl wrote it,
Józef Wilkoń painted the pictures
and Marion Koenig retold the story in English

North-South Books

NEW YORK   LONDON

LONG, LONG AGO a wolf lived in a great forest. He had learned from his father and grandfather that it was a wolf's duty to keep the forest in order. If even a little hare ventured out at night into the open, the wolf showed his teeth and snarled so fiercely that the hare was terrified and quickly hid in the thicket.

One night the owl left his nest in a high tree and flew down to the wolf. He rolled his big golden eyes and said: "All the animals are afraid of you. It would be better if they loved you for being clever, as they do me. What's the good of snarling and showing your teeth? You ought to go out into the world and learn to behave better."

The wolf thought about what the owl had said, and felt sad. "He is right," he decided. "I ought to go away." So he left the forest and moved into a cave a long way to the south to start a new way of life.

He began to do a number of very strange, unwolf-like things. He picked flowers, gathered berries, dried herbs and watched birds.

The animals who lived in those regions shook their heads. They thought he had gone mad. Of course, no one dared to say so out loud.

The wolf had hardly gone when the owl called a meeting and announced the good news. "Now there is nothing to be afraid of," he shrieked. "We can all do as we like."

"Fine," thought the fox, and snapped up a hen.

The owl was right. From now on everyone did as he pleased, and there was no more peace in the forest. The fierce animals enjoyed themselves, but the timid and gentle ones were terrified.

The wind went on howling and more snow fell. The paths were completely hidden under the snow and the animals became desperate. They huddled in holes in the snow and felt bitterly cold and hungry.

Even the fox became ill. He complained of dreadful pains in his inside, for his eyes had definitely been bigger than his stomach. But in spite of their misery, nobody dared to consult Doctor Wolf.

He sat in his surgery and waited. "They're still afraid of me," he thought. "And the owl only makes them feel worse. What can I do? I can't force them to come to me." Then he grew angry. "All right! Stay where you are," he shouted. "I'll go away."

He packed his bags and set off on his journey. He had almost reached the edge of the forest when he saw a very small rabbit huddled in the snow. It lay there, too hungry and frozen to move. Only its long ears twitched.

"There's no time to lose," said the wolf. He picked up the little rabbit and carried it back to his home. He tucked it up in his own warm bed and made a strong brew of hot camomile tea and honey.

In no time at all the little rabbit was well again. How happy it felt—and how ashamed! Was this the fierce wolf who ate up helpless rabbits? It shuffled its feet, thanked the wolf shyly, kissed his paw and bounded away to tell all the other animals what had happened.

When he heard what the rabbit had to say, the owl grew very excited. "The leopard does not change his spots," he screeched. "Once a wolf, always a wolf! He let the rabbit go free in order to lure us into his lair. . . ."

He paused, expecting the fox to agree with him, but the fox only groaned. "I've got such a pain in my stomach," he moaned. "I don't care what anyone says. Just take me to Doctor Wolf."

There aren't many stories in which a rabbit takes a fox to visit a wolf, but that's what happened in this one.

The wolf looked the fox over from head to foot. He prodded him in the stomach and said: "My friend, you are much too greedy. You eat too much. I'm putting you on a vegetarian diet. That means no more meat—just porridge or maize, and apples, pears, plums, carrots, cherries . . ."

The fox felt so ill that he promised never to eat another piece of meat as long as he lived. Then the wolf tucked the fox up in bed and put a hot compress on his stomach.

After that all the animals in the forest believed in the wolf's kindness and wisdom, and if any of them became ill, they ran straight to his surgery to be cured.

Only the owl still felt uneasy. He kept repeating: "Once a wolf, always a wolf, you mark my words," but nobody listened to him.

As for the fox, he was a much healthier animal on his new diet. He never learned to like salads, although, in time, he became quite fond of cherries and apples and pears and carrots.

Doctor Wolf eventually took a partner into his practice, and the two wolves could be seen on any fine day picking flowers and collecting herbs for their healing medicines.

Published in the United States, Great Britain, Canada,
Australia, and New Zealand by North-South Books,
an imprint of Nord-Süd Verlag AG, Gossau Zürich, Switzerland.

Distributed in the United States by North-South Books Inc., New York.

Library of Congress Cataloging-in-Publication Data
Nickl, Peter
The story of the kind wolf / by Peter Nickl ; illustrated by
Józef Wilkoń; translated and retold by Marion Koenig
Summary: A gentle wolf returns to the forest of his birth to practice
medicine, but a silly owl warns sick animals to stay away.
ISBN 1-55858-066-2 (HARDCOVER)
ISBN 1-55858-058-1 (PAPERBACK)
[1. Wolves—Fiction. 2. Owls—Fiction.]
I. Wilkoń, Józef, ill. II. Title.
PZ7.N5582 St 1982
82-670149

British Library Cataloguing in Publication Data
Nickl, Peter
The story of the kind wolf.
1. Title 11. Wilkoń, Józef
111. Die Geschichte vom guten Wolf
English
833'.914[J] PZ7

3 5 7 9 HC 10 8 6 4 2
3 5 7 9 PB 10 8 6 4 2
Printed in Belgium